Hansel and Gretel

Cover illustrated by
Angela Jarecki

Adapted by
Sarah Toast

Illustrated by
Susan Spellman

Louis Weber, C.E.O.
Publications International, Ltd.
7373 North Cicero Avenue
Lincolnwood, Illinois 60712

www.pubint.com

Manufactured in China.

8 7 6 5 4 3 2 1

ISBN: 0-7853-7872-3

Long ago a poor woodcutter lived on the outskirts of a large forest along with his family. He had two young children called Hansel and Gretel. The children's loving mother had died, and the stepmother did not like children.

When hard times came and even the rich had little, the woodcutter's family had nothing at all. At last the woodcutter said, "How can we possibly manage to feed our poor children when there isn't even enough for ourselves?"

His wife answered, "Well, we must take the children into the woods and leave them there to take care of themselves. That way maybe we will all have a chance. Otherwise, all four of us will starve."

Hansel heard his parents talking. When he told Gretel what he had heard, she cried.

"How can we manage alone in the woods?" she wept.

"Hush, Gretel," said Hansel. "We'll think of something."

That night Hansel waited until his parents were asleep. Then he crept carefully out of the house and filled his pockets with white stones.

The next morning the parents woke up the children and told them they had to come with them deep into the forest to gather wood. The stepmother handed them each a small piece of bread to nibble on, and off they went. Hansel lagged behind, dropping stones on the ground from time to time.

When the family was deep in the forest, the woodcutter started a fire to keep the children warm throughout the night.

"Eat your bread and then lie down by the warm fire," said the stepmother. "Your father and I will be back soon, after we have finished cutting wood."

The children were so tired that they fell fast asleep after they ate. When they awoke, they were alone in the dark.

"How will we ever get out of this forest?" cried Gretel. But Hansel told her that when the moon came up, they would find their way home. Sure enough, the bright moon shining on the white stones pointed them toward the path back home.

The tired children reached their cottage at daybreak. Their father was very happy to see them. He had sold the firewood for a good price, so for a while there was enough to eat.

But hard times soon came again. Early one morning, the children were again led into the forest with only a crust of bread.

"Don't worry, Gretel," said Hansel. "I have left a trail of breadcrumbs so we can find our way back."

Hansel and Gretel slept until the moon rose and then set out to find the trail. But alas, the hungry birds of the forest had eaten up every crumb. The poor children were truly lost.

Hansel and Gretel walked all night and all the next day. When they awoke from sleep the third day, they were almost too weak to walk anymore.

Gretel looked up and saw a beautiful white bird sitting on a branch. The bird sang to the children, and then it flew on ahead.

The children followed the white bird to an amazing little house made of gingerbread and candy. The hungry children broke off a piece of the house and began to eat. Their mouths were full of food when they heard a sweet and gentle voice:

"Nibble, nibble, like a mouse.
Who is nibbling at my house?"

The door opened and an old, old woman hobbled out. She came along slowly because she couldn't see very well.

The children were very frightened, but the old woman said, "You poor hungry children. Come in and I will give you better food."

The old woman gave Hansel and Gretel a large meal of pancakes and apples and milk. Then the kind old woman put them to sleep in soft beds under warm covers. They slept wonderfully, never guessing that the woman who seemed so nice was really wicked. She had built her house of cakes and candies to attract children so she could eat them!

The next morning the old woman dragged Hansel to a wooden cage and locked him in. Then she woke up Gretel.

"Fetch some water and make dumplings," she told the girl. "Fatten up your brother for me to eat!"

Gretel began to cry. The wicked old woman ignored Gretel's tears and made her cook and clean all day long.

Every morning the old woman told Hansel to hold out his finger so she could feel how fat he was growing. But Hansel knew that the old woman could not see well, so he held out an old bone for her to feel. This made her believe Hansel was still too thin to eat.

After four weeks Hansel didn't seem to be any fatter. But the old woman decided to eat him anyway and Gretel as well.

She told the girl to climb into the big oven to see if it was hot enough to bake bread. But Gretel, who knew better than to get into the oven, said she didn't know how.

"Foolish girl," said the wicked old woman. She leaned into the oven to show Gretel how to get into the oven. Gretel knew just what to do. She gave the old woman a big shove that sent her all the way into the back of the oven. Then Gretel shut the oven door and ran to free Hansel.

"Hansel, we're saved! The mean old woman is dead!" cried Gretel. She unlocked Hansel's cage, and they hugged each other and danced around the room.

Then the two children stuffed their pockets with jewels they found in boxes in the house. When they left, they took food with them.

After hours of walking, Hansel and Gretel came to a wide lake. Gretel called to a white swan, who agreed to take the children across. Across the lake, Hansel and Gretel soon found the path for home. When they saw their own house and their father, they began to run.

The woodcutter laughed and cried with joy to see his children again. He had been very sad since his evil wife had made him leave them in the forest. After his wife died, he searched for the children day and night.

The jewels would buy food for the rest of their days. Their worries were over, and the family lived happily.